Christmas in Lagos

BY **SHARON ABIMBOLA SALU**

ILLUSTRATED BY **MARIA NIKLA**

For My Family:
With You Every Christmas is Special
— S. A. S

A cold, dry wind blew in from the Sahara desert . . .

. . . and into
Ranti's room.

This was Harmattan,
which meant
one thing:
CHRISTMAS
was on
its way.

As she got ready for school, Ranti's younger brother, Debo, rushed into her room. "Ten days till Christmas!" he yelled.

DEC 15

Ranti was excited too. Christmas meant new clothes and shoes.

It was the last day of school. Miss Ani, the class teacher, asked the students to share what they planned to do over the Christmas holidays.

Some of Ranti's classmates were going abroad with their families and called out all the far-away places they would visit.

said Kamsi.

said Ladipo.

said Hauwa.

Ranti said nothing.

"What about you, Ranti?" Miss Ani asked.

Ranti did not want to speak up.

She imagined her classmates . . .

going ice skating,

building frosty snowmen,

eating tasty chocolates and taking fancy pictures.

Kamsi would visit
Times Square.

Ladipo would visit
Buckingham Palace.

Hauwa would see
the Eiffel Tower.

What about
Ranti?

There was no snow in Lagos, no tower to see, nothing exciting to do.

"This will be the most boring Christmas ever!" she told Miss Ani.

"No. Christmas in Lagos is very special. Open your eyes and look closer."

"But how?" Ranti asked.

"Write down everything that happens over the Christmas holidays," said Miss Ani.

So, Ranti got a journal and started writing. On December 16, she wrote:

Mummy took me to Balogun market today. It was very hot. People were everywhere, walking very fast. I didn't like the noise from cars or people shouting.

But I liked the Christmas songs playing on the radio. Mummy bought me and Debo new clothes and shoes. We can't wear them till Christmas. I can't wait!

On December 17, she wrote:

We passed by the airport today. Daddy said the aeroplanes are full of people coming to Lagos for Christmas.

Grandma and Grandpa came from Abeokuta this afternoon. I was so happy, I ran and hugged them! They will be spending Christmas with us.

Grandma said I looked taller. I told her I've been eating lots of beans.

After dinner, Grandpa told us the story of how the lion became King of the Jungle. I love his stories!

On December 18, she wrote:

We went to the amusement park today. Guess what? I saw Father Christmas! He gave me a toy puppy. Debo got a toy train. I want a real puppy, but Mummy said not yet.

After lunch, we visited an orphanage
and gave food and clothes to the children.
I gave a small girl my toy puppy
because she was crying.
Debo put his train
in his pocket.

CLOTHES

BEANS

GARRI

RICE

On December 19, she wrote:

Auntie Lola got married today. She looked so beautiful!

We ate lots of food and danced. On the way home,

I saw bright billboards . . .

and Christmas lights. I wish I could see them every day.

On December 20, she wrote:
Our neighbor, Mrs. Joseph has a dog
called Daisy.

Today, Daisy
gave birth to eight puppies!
Mrs. Joseph let me carry
one of them. It licked my face.
Mummy says I take good care
of Debo. I'm sure I could
take care of a puppy too.

On December 22, she wrote:
Today, we went to church for a Christmas Concert. The choir sang special Christmas songs in different languages.

Then, we lit candles and sang carols.

Finally, they lit a h-u-u-u-g-e Christmas tree. I loved it!

POP!
POP!
POP!

Finally, Christmas Day came.
The sounds of banger* and fireworks
filled the air. Everyone was excited.
Christmas was here
at last.

*firecrackers

Ranti wore her new dress and shoes.
Then she twirled . . .

and twirled . . .

and twirled . . .

. . . until she felt dizzy.

She loved her new outfit.
It made her feel special.

The whole family
went to church
that morning.

"We celebrate the birth of Jesus today," said the Pastor. "God gave Jesus, His best gift to mankind because He loves us. Spread love and joy this season."

Ranti wrapped her arms around her family
and whispered: "I love you."
"We love you too," they chorused.
After church, they went home, and celebrated
Christmas with . . .

. . . plates piled high with jollof rice, fried plantains, chicken, suya and other goodies.

Throughout the day, people came to visit.
Everyone had something to eat and drink.

They wished
each other . . .

**Merry
Christmas**

and

**Happy New
Year**

in advance!

Just before sunset, Mrs. Joseph arrived. In her arms, she carried a little puppy.

"This is for you, Ranti," she said.

"A real puppy! Thank you, ma!" Ranti squealed.

To the puppy, she whispered:

"I think I'll call you Tickles."

He yelped.

Before going to bed, Ranti wrote in her diary.

December 25:

Today was the best Christmas ever! I wore my
new dress and shoes and ate lots of food.
Guess what? I have a puppy! A real one, not a toy.
He's so cute and cuddly!
But what I really enjoyed . . .

. . . *was spending time with my family.*

On the first day
back at school, Ranti read her
Christmas journal to the class.
Everyone clapped.

Thank you, Miss Ani.
"had the best Christmas
ever!" said Ranti.
Miss Ani smiled.
"I knew you would."

THANK YOU FOR READING

I hope you enjoyed reading this story.
If you did, I would really appreciate
a short review on Amazon
or your favorite book website.
Reviews make a big difference!
Thank you for your support.

More exciting stories
for your library

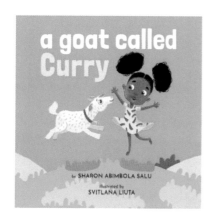

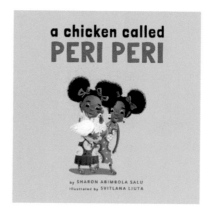

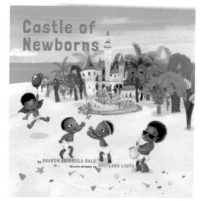

ABOUT THE AUTHOR

Sharon Abimbola Salu is the author of three picture books: **A Goat Called Curry, A Chicken Called Peri Peri** and **Castle of Newborns.** Born and raised in Lagos, Nigeria, she now lives in the United States of America. Visit **SharonSalu.com**.

ABOUT THE ILLUSTRATOR

Maria Nikla is an illustrator from Athens, Greece. She holds a Bachelor of Arts degree in Illustration from the University of Brighton. Maria resides in Brighton, United Kingdom.

Made in the USA
Middletown, DE
17 December 2020